TALES FROM INDIA

Retold by
Sanjeevini, Navjeet
and Misti

Illustrated by Daksha Patel
and Manju Gregory

(The Four Friends)

For Arjun, Kunal and Christopher

Introduction

For over two thousand years mythological and folk tales have been told and retold, sung, enacted and danced in every Indian village and market place. These have been enjoyed by the young and old, not only for their story-line but also as guides to morality and wisdom. The purpose of our Rajarani Series is to introduce these stories to children using an exciting combination of powerful illustrations and the spoken word. We hope also that Indian parents, who may have forgotten the finer details, can enjoy these tales with their children and continue an age old tradition.

Text © 1984. Mantra Publishing Ltd.
Illustrations © 1984 Daksha Patel
Calligraphy Manju Gregory,

British Library Cataloguing in Publication Data
Dutta, Sanjeevini
    Tales from India.—(Rajarani series; pt.1)
    1. Tales—India
    I. Title   II. Chatterji, Mishti
    III. Singh, Navjeet   IV. Patel, Daksha
    V. Gregory, Manju   VI. Series
398.2'1'0954 PZ8.1
ISBN 0–947679–00–6
Address: Mantra Publishing Ltd,
                17F Church Crescent,
                London N10 3NA, U.K.
Printed by: Blantyre Printing & Binding Co. Ltd, Blantyre, Glasgow.

Contents

Akbar and Birbal: The Journey to Heaven

The court of King Akbar, the great Emperor, was famous for its musicians, poets and wise people of all kinds. Amongst them was Birbal who was the King's cleverest minister. He was also Akbar's best friend. This made the nobles of the court extremely jealous and they were always secretly plotting against him.

One day they had an idea: "Let us ask the King's Barber to help us. He is often alone with the King. Besides, Akbar trusts him completely."

So they approached the Barber. "We need your help, O royal Barber. Birbal poisons the King's mind against us. We must get rid of him."

"But...." hesitated the Barber.

"We will repay you well," said one courtier quickly. "If you help us you will never need to do another day's work in your life!"

The Barber, who was a lazy and greedy man, said to himself: "What do I care about these petty, squabbling courtiers," and at the prospect of no more work and a life full of comfort, he said: "Leave it to me. I shall think of a plan."

A little while later, as he shaved Akbar, he said to the King: "Sire, don't you ever wonder what your beloved father is doing in the next world?"

"Don't be foolish my man!" snapped Akbar. "How can I or anyone know what is happening in the world beyond?"

"Well, you could send someone there to find out," the Barber continued cautiously.

"What a stupid idea," said Akbar in annoyance. "To reach the other world my messenger would have to die first."

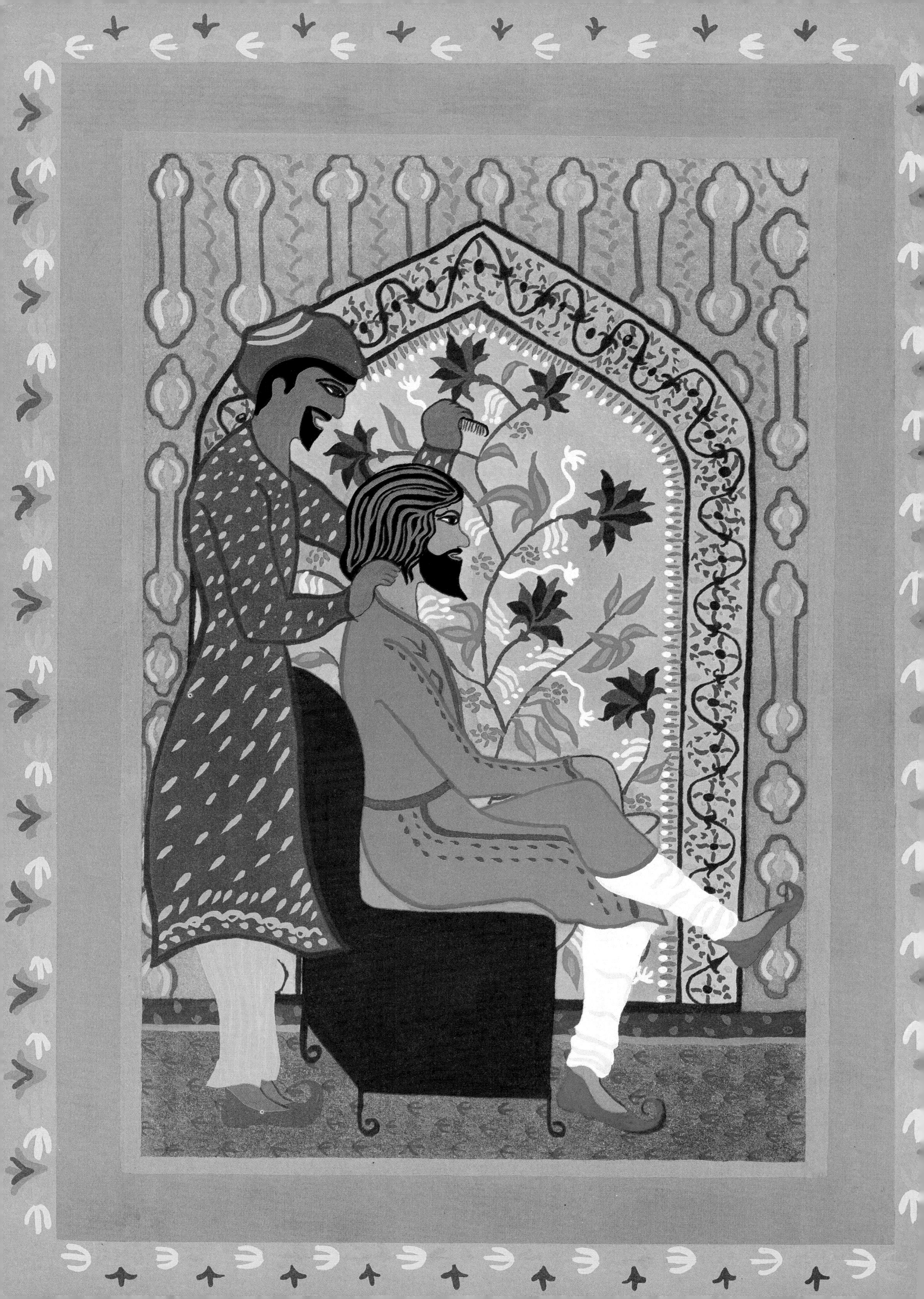

"No your Majesty, not necessarily," the Barber said quickly. "There is another way — the magical way!" Akbar's curiosity was aroused. Encouraged, the Barber said: "In the forest, on the edge of the city, lives an old magician. He has such powers that he can send people flying through the air into the next world. He simply puts them on a funeral pyre and they rise with the smoke to heaven."

Akbar was doubtful. "And can he bring the messenger back as well?"

"Easily, your Majesty," the Barber replied. "By repeating the magic spell backwards!" Akbar was intrigued. The Barber continued: "However a word of warning. The journey to heaven is full of dangers. If he is to be successful the messenger must tread very carefully. He must be very clever."

"Well, do you have any ideas?" asked the King.

The Barber carefully made his master move. "The wisest man in the kingdom is Birbal, your Majesty."

"Ah," said Akbar to himself, "Birbal's enemies are up to their tricks again. But let us see how Birbal gets out of this one." Turning to the Barber with a smile, he agreed: "Yes of course, Birbal must be our man."

The Barber was overjoyed; his scheme had worked! Birbal was summoned and told of his mission. He realised at once that this was a plot but quickly countered with a plan. "Your Majesty, I must be suitably dressed for this long and important journey," he said. "I must also select the choicest gifts from our world to present to your father. All this will take a little time." Akbar agreed and a date was fixed.

Birbal acted quickly. He immediately began digging a long winding tunnel from his house, under the narrow streets, beneath the marble palace, and up to the grounds where the funeral pyre was being prepared.

When the tunnel was completed Birbal arrived at court and declared that he was ready for his journey to heaven. He was placed upon the pyre and the Barber, now disguised as the magician, lit it much to the glee of the waiting courtiers.

As the thick smoke screened Birbal from the onlookers, he quickly moved the logs covering the entrance to his secret tunnel and crawled safely home. He remained indoors, making sure that nobody saw him. He was also careful not to shave or cut his hair.

Time passed. Yet there was no sign of Birbal. Akbar grew restless and worried. Perhaps the mission was beyond even wise Birbal. Just when he had given up all hope, Birbal suddenly appeared. The courtiers gasped in disbelief. But Akbar was thrilled.

"Birbal! Thank God you are safe! How is my father? Is he well?"

"He is in excellent spirits your Majesty. But he did have one request," replied Birbal.

"Go on," said the King.

"Well, he did say it was not very important," hesitated Birbal.

"What is it? Whatever he needs he shall have."

"Your Majesty," replied Birbal, "as you can see from my long hair and untidy beard, there are no barbers in heaven. Your father requests, if it is not too much trouble, that you send him a really good barber."

"Of course, of course. We can't have him looking scruffy and unshaven. I will send my personal Barber. Pack your bags immediately," Akbar ordered the Barber. "You are to go on a long journey to attend to my father."

The courtiers were stunned. They thought they had seen the end of Birbal, but now realised that he had taken his revenge. They did not dare plot against him for a long, long time. As for the poor Barber, he could see no way out, for after all it was his own idea.

Jataka: The Deer and the King

In the forest, beyond the city of Benares, lived many beautiful deer. Their leader stood out above the rest: his coat was dusky gold, his body sleek as a dart and his eyes gleamed like rubies. He was always reminding his herd to be alert to the sound of distant drums, as that meant danger!

The King of Benares was a hunter who killed deer for food and pleasure. Every week, he would order his subjects to join him in the hunt. The sport began with a noisy beating of drums as the mob marched into the silent forest. The frightened deer would flee desperately away, only to be trapped by a shower of arrows from the King lying in wait on the other side.

Many arrows would find their targets but only one or two would kill. The dead deer would be taken to the castle for feasting while the many wounded suffered a slow, painful death.

"This cannot go on," said the leader one day. "If we have to die, so be it; but let us not be left crippled." The herd agreed. They decided that it was far better for one deer to sacrifice himself for the sake of the others. They would draw straws from a bundle of hay. The deer who drew the shortest straw would have to stand still and offer himself as target, while the rest fled to safety.

One day, before yet another hunt, a doe with a newly born fawn drew the shortest straw. She was terrified for her child and pleaded with the leader: "Master, today it is my turn to die. My fawn is still young and unable to feed herself. If I die who will take care of her? I beg you, free me this time and later, when my child is older, I shall gladly fulfil my duty."

"I cannot order another to take your place," replied the leader. "Yet, I understand your fear. Go, protect your little one."

As the sound of the hunters pierced through the forest, the leader quietly left the herd and made his way towards the castle.

The King had already mounted his horse and was about to leave when a bewildered guard rushed to him. "Majesty!" he cried. "A golden deer is at the castle gate, erect as a noble, looking like a God!"

The King saw the beautiful deer staring at him, awaiting death. He dismounted thoughtfully and walking up to the deer, said gently: "My friend, O leader, why are you here?"

"Great King, a doe in my herd was due to stand as target today, but begged to be spared for the sake of her infant. I as leader, could not order another to take her place. That is why I am here."

The King said in wonder: "Golden deer, I have never seen such an act of self- sacrifice, not even amongst men. Go, return in peace."

"You have spared my life Great King, but what of my herd?"

"Great Deer, I spare their lives as well."

"Sire, you have spared the deer, but what of the other animals?"

"I spare their lives too."

"Great King, the animals will be safe. What of the birds in your kingdom?"

"The birds shall be spared, and so will the fish in the rivers and the lakes."

The golden deer thanked the King and returned to the forest to spend the rest of his life in peace.

Folktale: The Four Friends

Once upon a time, in a small town, there lived four friends. They had known each other from childhood and spent much of their time together. Three of the friends were very proud of their knowledge; they had studied many subjects and felt that they knew everything. The fourth friend, Gopal, had not read *as* many books as his learned friends, but possessed a great deal of common sense.

One day the friends were discussing their future. "I suggest that the time has come for us to prove ourselves and make our fortune," said the first friend. "There is nothing to be gained by staying on in this town."

"We must travel to distant lands," agreed the second, "and meet important people who will pay us well to answer difficult questions."

"That's a good idea!" said the third friend. "We may even win the favour of kings and become very powerful. Let us leave without further delay."

The first friend suddenly pointed with annoyance at Gopal and said: "How can we call ourselves the world's most learned if we have this ignorant fellow with us. I suggest we leave him behind."

The second friend agreed: "Indeed, he would only spoil our chances if he came with us. There is no use in taking him."

"We cannot do that!" protested the third friend. "We have all been friends for a long time and have done everything together. We must take him with us."

So the next day all four started on their journey. They walked the whole day till at nightfall they reached a thick forest. Suddenly, the first friend tripped over what appeared to be the bones of a dead animal.

"Wait! Here is an ideal opportunity to test our knowledge. Let us bring this skeleton to life. I, with my vast knowledge," he continued proudly, "know how to put the bones together."

The second friend quickly added: "And I know how to provide the skin, flesh and blood."

"But only I," interrupted the third friend, "can put the breath of life into the animal!"

So the first friend arranged all the bones and the second supplied the skin, flesh and blood. The third friend was just about to bring the beast to life when Gopal shouted: "STOP! Do you clever men realise just what you are creating? This is a lion. You can't possibly bring it back to life!"

"Of course I can!" scoffed the third friend. "I can and I shall. Just you watch!"

"Then please wait. Give me a few minutes to climb a tree," said Gopal as he scaled up a huge banyan tree.

The third friend then gave the magic spell: "JANTRAMANTRA, arise O lion." Life slowly entered the dead beast. First his tail twitched. Then his body stirred and his head shook.

"Hoorah!" said the friends, congratulating one another. "We have done it!" Suddenly the lion sprang up with a mighty growl. The terrified friends gasped in disbelief and fled in all directions as the lion gave chase.

Gopal could only look down in horror. When all was clear he climbed down the tree and hurried home. He waited anxiously for the others. They arrived late the next day, shaken and exhausted. No mention was made of the incident. But from that day on the three learned men always listened to the advice of their friend, Gopal.

MAHABHARATA: The Story of BHEEM

Many years ago, there lived in North India, five famous princes and their hundred wicked cousins. The five, known as the Pandavs, were Bheem the strong, Yudhisthir the wise, Arjun the warrior and the twins, Nakul and Sahadev. They lost their father, the King of Hastinapura, when they were still children and too young to rule. Their blind uncle was crowned instead. He had a hundred sons called the Kauravs.

As children, the Pandavs and their cousins, the Kauravs, were brought up together in the palace where they learnt archery, fencing, wrestling and other arts of warfare. Although they studied and played together they did not like each other. Duryodhan, the eldest Kaurav, was jealous of his popular and talented cousins. He knew that the Pandavs were the rightful heirs to the throne and that as long as they were alive he would never be king. He hated Bheem in particular, who always defeated him in games and tests of strength. Every time Bheem won, Duryodhan became more angry and unhappy until he hated Bheem with such passion that he decided to kill him. He went to his evil uncle, Sakuni, and told him of his wish to get rid of Bheem. Together they hatched a wicked plot.

One lovely winter's day Sakuni told all the children that he had arranged a royal picnic on the banks of a river by the hills. There would be plenty of delicious food, curried with many different spices, and even wild boar if they could catch one in the forest nearby. The princes were thrilled! They spent the morning hunting, playing games and telling each other stories. By mid-day, when they were tired and hungry, they settled down to a grand feast.

As usual Bheem was the hungriest and ate the most. Sakuni watched with delight for, unknown to anyone, he had poisoned Bheem's food with a powerful potion.

After the meal the princes lay down contented and one by one drifted off to sleep. Duryodhan and Sakuni waited as Bheem fell into a deep slumber. When they were sure everyone was fast asleep they quickly tied Bheem's arms and legs and threw him into the river.

Many vicious and deadly snakes lived in the river. They hissed with delight and bit Bheem over and over again as he sank to the bottom. Then a strange thing happened. Their venom only killed Sakuni's poison in Bheem so that he awoke. Finding his arms and legs tied and the snakes attacking him Bheem was enraged! In his fury he ripped apart the ropes that shackled him and turned on the snakes with a vengeance, twisting their necks until they choked to death. He killed so many that the rest of the snakes fled in terror.

The Snake King had watched this fierce contest. He was very impressed. "Who is this man," he said to himself, "that despite our bites, still lives and attacks us?" He called out to Bheem: "You are the most courageous man I have ever seen! My snakes are wicked. They bite anyone unfortunate enough to fall into the water. But to this day no one has dared fight back as you did. You have taught them a lesson they will never forget and, as a reward, I will make you the strongest man in the world."

The Snake King invited Bheem to his underwater palace. He led him to a huge cavern filled with hundreds of bowls. "These bowls contain a magic broth," he said. "Drink as many as you wish, for each bowl will give you the strength of a thousand elephants."

Bheem was thrilled. He drank eagerly for the fight with the snakes had made him very thirsty. After the eighth bowl he lay down satisfied and fell fast asleep. Eight days later he awoke feeling refreshed and stronger than ever before. Thanking the Snake King he swam to the bank and walked back to Hastinapura.

Bheem's brothers, who had given him up for dead, were overjoyed to see him. His mother embraced him with great relief and happiness. Duryodhan however was furious. He had thought that his enemy was destroyed but Bheem had returned even more powerful. Duryodhan could not bear it and vowed not to rest until he had killed all the Pandav brothers.

Panchatantra: The Donkey has no Brains

Sher Shah the lion, king of the forest, groaned with pain. His stomach made strange sounds. The sad fact was that he was growing old and weak. The weaker he grew, the slower he ran; the slower he ran, the less food he caught. Now, even goats and donkeys escaped his attacks. Sher Shah, king of the forest, could no longer even feed himself.

Something had to be done. He needed food or he would die. "Yes, that's it, Sher Shah you clever old lion," he said to himself. "You must get yourself an assistant. The cunning little fox will be the perfect choice."

He called the fox sweetly: "Dearest friend, I have always admired your great wisdom and knowledge. I would like to make you my second in command. You shall be in charge of policing the forest." Of course the fox did not believe him, as Sher Shah continued grandly: "Your first duty shall be to advise on law and order. You shall report all cases of animals breaking the law and suggest suitable punishments. Secondly," and here the lion hesitated, "you shall provide all my meals. It is not fit, not dignified, for the king to run after his dinner."

The fox now realised what was on the lion's mind but felt that he had no choice. "I will do my best to serve your Highness," he said as he went off in search of the lion's first meal.

A while later he met a foolish donkey. "Great news, O donkey," he said, "you have been honoured, greatly honoured."

"Honoured?" queried the puzzled donkey.

"Yes. Hon-our-ed," repeated the fox. "In recognition of your well-known courage and wisdom, Sher Shah our king, has chosen you as his grand Vazir. He awaits your presence impatiently."

The poor donkey was bewildered: "The lion.... but he only wants to eat me."

"Nonsense my friend, you are much too modest," flattered the fox. "He values your loyalty too much to waste it by eating you."

"But the last time I met him…." persisted the donkey doubtfully.

"You worry too much," interrupted the fox. "Just come with me and see the grand reception the king has prepared for you."

The donkey was completely confused. But he was also thrilled with the fox's flattery — at last his qualities were being recognised. His suspicions lulled, he went along with the fox to the lion's den. But as they approached, the old doubts arose once again and the donkey stopped short. The fox called out slyly: "Your grand Vazir is here, your Highness, but he is feeling shy and refuses to come up close to you."

"I understand perfectly," replied the lion. "His modesty pleases me greatly. I shall go to him myself." But the sight of the approaching lion struck such terror in the donkey that he bolted away in haste, leaving behind a very hungry Sher Shah.

"You bungler!" accused the lion. "If you do not bring back that juicy donkey by sunset I shall have your measly body for dinner, be sure of it."

The fox was annoyed. "I shall try again," he said. "But with respect, it was your great haste that scared the donkey. This time will you please let me bring him a little closer." Muttering under his breath the fox set off in search once again.

When he met the donkey he said, "What a strange animal you are. Don't you wish to be made the grand Vazir?"

"But suppose he kills me!" blurted out the donkey.

"If he wanted to, he could easily have killed you by now," replied the fox, trying to calm the donkey's fears again. "My friend, it is clear that he wants you as an ally, not as a victim. You will be the most powerful animal in the forest, second only to the king. Everyone will look up to you and beg you for favours." The donkey was pleased at the thought of his new role and power. He was now convinced that the fox was telling the truth.

He followed the fox back to the lion's cave. This time however, Sher Shah did not move, even though he was twice as hungry as before. He welcomed the donkey. "I pronounce you my grand Vazir for life! Now we must discuss urgent affairs of state. Come closer my friend." As the donkey reached within striking distance, the lion pounced swiftly, killing him with one mighty blow on the head.

Happily licking his lips, he thanked the fox and turned to his long-awaited dinner. But the fox was hungry too after all his efforts. He quickly said: "Your Highness, it is only right that in true royal tradition, the king should bathe before the feast." The lion was pleased, he liked being recognised as royalty. Instructing the fox to guard the dead donkey, he hurried off to bathe.

The fox was angry. It was most unfair, he thought, that the lion should enjoy the feast when he had done all the work and deserved the juiciest piece. He quickly tore open the donkey's head and ate the delicious brain.

When the lion returned he immediately noticed that the head had been cut open. He growled at the fox: "Did you do this?" The fox pretended to be deeply hurt and said: "Your Highness, how could I? It was your powerful blow that split open the head. Surely you remember that?"

The fox's innocent look satisfied Sher Shah, who once again turned to his dinner. Almost instantly he roared: "Where is the brain? His brain is missing. I wanted to eat *that* first; it is my favourite piece."

"Your Highness, Sire," pleaded the fox. "Please calm down. Surely you are aware that donkeys have no brains. If this one did, do you think he would have come back a second time?"

"Hmm.... I suppose you are right," agreed the lion and happily munched his long-awaited dinner.

Notes and Sources

AKBAR BIRBAL

Akbar was a Mughal Emperor who ruled from 1560 till 1605. The Mughals were Muslims who came from Central Asia and ruled India for over 200 years. Akbar was a patron of the Arts and a philosopher. He was also highly respected for his fair treatment of his Hindu subjects. This story is one of several about Akbar and his Hindu minister, Birbal, which although difficult to authenticate have nevertheless become legendary.

Pyre: a pile of wood for burning a corpse. Hindus are cremated on death.

JATAKA

The Jataka is a collection of stories about the 580 previous lives of the Buddha. In each story he appears in the form of a man or an animal to preach Buddhist principles. It is said that the Buddha himself narrated these stories to his disciples in the sixth century B.C. Murals depicting the Jataka stories can be found in the Ajanta caves in Western India.

MAHABHARATA

The Mahabharata is one of the most famous Indian epics and possibly the longest poem in the world. It dates back to 500 B.C. and contains much of the mythology and religion of the Hindus. It works on two levels: as a human drama, it is a story of the feud between two branches of a family which leads to a mighty war. At the same time it is also a guide to religion and morality. The Bhagavad Gita, the sacred book of the Hindus, is contained in the Mahabharata.

PANCHATANTRA

The Panchatantra are ancient fables which can be traced back to 200 B.C. These take a worldly view and stress the art of practical living.

Vazir: a Minister.
Banyan tree: a tree with spreading aerial roots commonly found in India.